W9-CFC-455

Just One Apple

Janosch

North
South

There was once a man named Walter; he was the poorest man in the whole kingdom. He had one apple tree. Its leaves were bright green, its bark was healthy, and its trunk was straight and strong. But the tree never bore any fruit—not a single apple.

When spring came, Walter stared sadly at everyone else's blossom-covered trees. There were hundreds of thousands of delicate white flowers shimmering in the sunlight. But his tree did not have a single blossom.

When autumn came, Walter stared sadly at everyone else's apple-covered trees. The branches were bending under their burden, and people across the kingdom were carrying home baskets full of fruit.

When Walter was in bed that night, he wished with all his heart for just one apple. *It needn't even be a very beautiful one,* he thought.

And his wish came true, as wishes sometimes do.

The next spring Walter saw a beautiful blossom on his tree. His eyes shone with joy, and he danced beneath the tree. From then on he guarded his blossom day and night.

When a cold wind blew from the mountain, Walter shielded the flower with his hands, and when the sun shone too fiercely, he shaded it.

During the summer the blossom grew into a little apple. Walter was happier than ever. His cheeks were red, his eyes were as clear as the summer sky, and his feet were as light as air. He felt that everyone in the kingdom was his friend.

As autumn came, the apple grew and grew. But when it was fruit-picking time, Walter decided to wait. With each passing day, the apple grew bigger and bigger.

Passersby would say: "Look at that apple. It ought to be eaten."

Soon Walter became afraid of thieves. He trusted no one—and even his friends deserted him.

At last Walter decided to pick the apple and take it to market. But he could not get the apple into the train because it was too wide for the doors. So he carried the heavy fruit all the way on his back. The weight was tremendous, but the thought of the high price he would get for the apple made him stagger on.

But in the market everyone scoffed at him: "You're a liar and a braggart! No one has ever seen such a huge apple. It can't possibly be real."

"Why don't you eat the apple yourself?" someone asked nastily.

Walter had to admit that he didn't like apples. Then everyone laughed at him until they got bored, and Walter found himself alone. He stood beside his apple, tired and dejected.

Walter continued to guard his apple day and night. But it no longer gave him any pleasure. He became thin and ill. Then something extraordinary happened.

A monstrous green dragon had descended upon the kingdom and was ruining the harvest and frightening everyone.

The king summoned his best detectives and said, "Get rid of that monster. Clap it in irons and get it out of the country."

But the dragon was too fierce. Then, just when it seemed hopeless, they remembered Walter and the big apple.

They knocked on his door: "We must take this apple. We're sorry, but we're acting in the king's name."

Walter made no protest. He was delighted that he would not have to guard his apple any longer.

The detectives pushed and pulled the gigantic apple to the gigantic dragon, and the greedy beast started to devour it. It stuffed and stuffed and stuffed itself, and had not even eaten half when it choked on it and fell down dead!

The detectives carted away the dragon. The king danced joyfully, and the whole country was saved.

Walter was happy again. His cheeks were as red as before, and he forgot all his troubles. But in bed that night he thought over what had happened, and this time he wished for two apples. *Two small apples that can be put into a basket and sold in the market*, he thought, then fell asleep happily.

Copyright © 1965 by NordSüd Verlag AG, CH-8005 Zürich, Switzerland.
First published in Switzerland under the title *Das Apfelmännchen*.
English translation copyright © 1966 by Dobson Books, Ltd.
English translation copyright © 1989 by NorthSouth Books Inc., New York 10016.

All rights reserved.
No part of this book may be reproduced or utilized in any form or by any means, electronic or mechanical, including photo-copying, recording, or any information storage and retrieval system, without permission in writing from the publisher.

This edition first published in the United States, Great Britain, Canada, Australia, and New Zealand in 2014 by NorthSouth Books, Inc., an imprint of NordSüd Verlag AG, CH-8005 Zürich, Switzerland.

Distributed in the United States by NorthSouth Books Inc., New York 10016.
Library of Congress Cataloging-in-Publication Data is available.
ISBN: 978-0-7358-4151-2 (trade edition)

Printed in Germany by Grafisches Centrum Cuno GmbH & Co. KG, Calbe, April 2014.
www.northsouth.com